The Muchly Fed Up Tortoise and More Nonsuch Poems

Florence Remmer

Published by PublishingPush.com

Acknowledgements

To my gold and emerald rock for your wonderful help

Thank you
Fairy Pearl

Contents

A Good Spree

An adventurous Dormouse
Resented the way
He was programmed to sleep
For most of the day
He yearned for adventure
Perhaps that's why he
Unprogrammed himself
And went off on a spree

He laughed in delight
As he whizzed into Town
Where he Twizzled and Whistled
And spun round and round
And Spreed and fast Spreed
'Til he fell in a heap
Then contentedly programmed
Himself back to sleep

All that Glisters

Hey up, that Magpie's zooming in
He's homing in to pilfer!
Lock away your Ruby Ring
Cover all your Silver

Hide your Green Glass baubles
In socks, that's my advice
Then wave two rings of Silver foil
To catch that robber's eyes

Yes, wave two rings of Silver foil
To glitter brightly in the sun,
All is glister to that Bird
He'll grab the foil and then fly on

Dear Google,...

...Can you tell me, do you know,
The place where Missing Socks all go?
I'm always losing one you see
It really is a mystery…..

WELL…..
The answer to your question
Is very, very clear
Socks don't go missing
They run away we fear

Now why and where they run to
We really do not know
But mostly they'll turn up again
Of that you can be sure

The Sulking Mouse

Four Mice live in a squarish field
They rent a quarter each
Three of them are neighbourly
The fourth stays out of reach

Three Mice are nice and neighbourly

A' running to and fro
The fourth sits sulking all day long
Why so?… we'd like to know!

'tis because I have a fixture
and the other three have not…
…'tis the Farmer's
Nosey Scarecrow
A'poled on my plot.!

In Praise of The English Channel

I was explaining to a Seagull,
One breezy Plymouth day
…about the English Channel,
In a prideful kind of way…

…about the lively Channel
Its briskly swelling Tides
Its choppy sometime stillness
Its unrivalled Maritime

About our guardful Channel
Full castled West to East
Its fearless Ancient Mariners
Its modern Matchless Fleet…

…of the Channel Tides that bore us safe
From those Dunkirk shores
The Channel winds that scattered
The Armada off its course,,,

Well,, the Seagull was astounded!
And he shed a briny tear
As he praised Our English Channel…
…his praise was music to my ear !

The Fears of the Bully Cat

"How many lives do you have left Tom?"
"Oh, I think about four…And you?"

"Well I'm not much good at counting
But I think my last one's due

Aye, I'm Moulting left and right lad
Too tired to Dash about

But the thing I dread the most Tom…
What if the Mice find out?"

"Oh if those vengeful pesky Mice catch on
That life will not be worth a penny, Tom"

A Muchly Fed Up Tortoise...

…grumbled at the way
Miss Mouse sat on his shelly back
To while the time away

It weren't so much
Her sitting there
As made the Tortoise grouse

No… 'twas when she
Started talking
In her squeaky little voice

And when she Started singing
And that squeak began to soar…

…Oh, that muchly
Fed up Tortoise
Grumbled even more.

Hat Shop

If you open a Hat Shop
To cater for Cats
Who come in their lunch breaks
To try on your Hats

O, if you start such a venture
Pray take my advice
And NEVER employ
Any Milliner Mice
No....

When Miss Cat tries a hat on
She don't want to see
Haute Couture Milliners
A'rolling in glee

Now, they may be proficient
And their work may impress
But Sniggering Mice they are
Nevertheless

The Horticultural Show

A Gardener Cat polished ten rosy apples
And wrapped them with care
For the Show the next day
A sly Mouse looked on and fuming with envy
Hatched up a plan
To spoil the display

Now everyone needs to be told they are wanted
Everyone needs
To furnish a home
The sly Mouse knew this and taking advantage
He offered ten Maggots
A place of their own

He offered the Maggots ten rosy red Homesteads
O, he carried their bags
And helped them move in
Then he hid in a tree
 in the Gardener Cats' garden
And waited 'til morn
For the fun to begin.

The Spiteful Catfish

A Castaway Mouse
(a Sailor by trade)
Spent his time writing "rescue me" notes

He set them in bottles
Then flung them to sea
In the hope they would reach rescue boats

He wasn't to know
His bottled up pleas
Drifted on to the Catfish Sea…
…and the Catfish spent hours
Reading his notes
Ere tearing them up in great glee. Spiteful

The Jealous Tadpole

A jealous little Tadpole sat
Beneath a Lily Crown
Watching Frogs and Insect things
Leaping up and down

Watching Insect things and Frogs
A'hopping to and fro
And wishing he could do the same
(Tadpoles can't, you know)

I told him to swim on until
He grew two legs… but he
Wept jealous 'neath the lily crown
And paid no heed to me.

A Tall Order

Dear fashion
Goo Roo,
Here's a question for you

Do you have the
Right answer?
Please share it…

…if I send
A Blue Necklace
To Mistress Giraffe

On which part
Of her neck
Should she wear it?

A Lesson Learnt

Every Child must go to school
This has always been the rule
Naughty Children stay away
"We'll go tomorrow, not today"
They say

But naughty Children are not wise
And quickly learn to their surprise
That Children, good, who go to school
Can read and write and spell, "you fool"
That's cool!

The Dream of Edna Rabbit

 If I had a Dream House
Where would it be?
Why right beneath
A Lettuce Patch
Yes, that's the Home for me!

With a hundred little Warrens
Running to and fro
And a hundred little
Trap Doors
Where the Lettuce grow! YUMMY

Long Long Ago......

Nine Bronze Age Cats sat down in a ring
A'practising deep meditation
They invited three curious Mice to join in
Who accepted their kind invitation.

Who accepted their kind invitation with thanks
And, obeying the Cats to the letter,
They all sat around in the ring holding hands
A'yinging and yanging together

A'yinging and yanging and swaying about
Heads bowed in a mystical wafting
A Cat began chanting in deep dulcet tone…
…and all of the Mice started laughing

'Twas then, when the mice began rolling in glee,
Fur flew, there was scratching and biting
So long long ago and O, ever since then
Cats and Mice have been feuding and fighting

Dawn Chorus

Bolton Woods May 1998
Down in the Woods
'Neath a dawny pink sky
The Choirs assemble
Excited and shy
Beaks open wide
And a song in their hearts
It's time for the May Time
Dawn Chorus to start

A Wren blows a whistle
An Owl nods his chin
A Lark begins singing
The Chorus joins in…
A' HERALDING SPRING !!!
It's MAY Time! It's MAY Time!
Begin oh Begin

O Begin! O Begin! O! Begin O! Begin
O let our sweet May Time
Dawn Chorus begin!!!

Elf 'N' Safety

A bored Tom Cat
A bored young Mouse
Sit mutely in
A boring house

No claws allowed!
No Micey grin!
No chasing out
Or chasing in

No slights are slung
No fight unfurled
What a Boring,
Sterile
    P.C. world!!!!!!!!!!!!

Puzzled by Magnetic Science

A Cat and a Mouse were having a fight
In a Boxing Ring,
Yes, doing it right
The Cat, all smiles, had slyly shoved
A lump of iron
Down his boxing glove

The Mouse, all grins, had read that Cat
And a magnet in
His right hand sat
As they faced each other in the Boxing Ring
A'waiting, grinning,
For the bell to ping.....

TELL ME
Would the magnet whiz that Cat
To a sharp right hook
And lay him flat?
Or would it be the Mouse that shot
Across the ring,
And a black eye got?

How To Deal With a Miscreant Mouse

(by a no nonsense Cat)

Lure him to the Waxworks
Turn the lights to "dim"
Open the Chamber of Horrors
And throw the Scoundrel in

Pay no heed to his yelling
His protests of foul play
Lock him up with Mummies and Co.
And throw the keys away!

Leave him until morning
Then throw him out the door
O! you will not see his heels for dust
Gone...For ever more. (Tee hee)

The Miserly Sparrow

A miserly Sparrow
Sat counting his crumbs
Watched by a Hungry Mouse
Sucking her thumbs

Watched by a Hungry Mouse
Sucking each thumb
And willing the Sparrow
To give her a crumb

Oh willing the Sparrow
To look up and see
A thumb sucking Hungry Mouse
Wanting her tea

But I'm sorry to say
There was nary a word
Nor the gift of a crumb
From that miserly Bird

A Compassionate Wasp...

...on discovering a sting
Is the most
Painful thing..

(He'd been stung
On the head
By a Gnat)...

...Leaves his own sting at home
Ere joining
The swarm

And you cannot
Do fairer
Than that!

The Mole and his New Digger (snigger)

A go-ahead Mole decided one day
To hone up his dig digging skill
So he traded his old trusty Spade in
For a shiny brand Pneumatic Drill

Oh! he couldn't contain his excitement
As he pressed on the thingy marked 'go'
(But ah! there's a line twixt an old trusty Spade...
...and a Pneumatic Drill, as you know)

As he naively gripped on the handle
The Drill gave an up and down dive,
Then set off at speed, like a piston
With the Mole clinging on for dear life
Now, I cannot say how his dig ended
As the last thing I heard from the Mole
Was a scream and a whoop as he vanished
Down a Pneumatised five fathom hole

The Window Seat

A Cat was travelling on a train
When to his great delight
Five Country Mice rolled down the aisle
Entangled in a fight

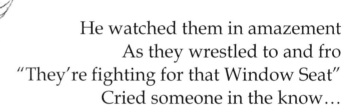

He watched them in amazement
As they wrestled to and fro
"They're fighting for that Window Seat"
Cried someone in the know…

"The Winner takes that Window Seat"
"No way", the Cat replied
Whence he leaped into THAT Window Seat
And sat there satisfied.

In Theory....

…a six fingered sloth
(Three on each hand)
Could play the piano, you know

Though his fingers can't reach
A full octave scan
He could tackle the me, re and doh

I'm aware that his tune
To refined ears would be
A monotonous sound to endure

Still, a six fingered sloth
(Three on each hand),
Could play the piano I'm sure.

Mother Sparrow Explains

Dear Mother Sparrow
Please answer me right…
…How do you kiss
Your babies Goodnight?

You do not have lips
You have only a beak?

> *"Well, they have to make do*
> *With a peck on the cheek*
>
> *"Yes a peck on the left*
> *And a peck on the right*
> *That's how I kiss*
> *My babies Goodnight*
>
> *"…and after their pecks*
> *They snuggle down deep*
> *Whilst I wrap my wings round them*
> *And sing them to sleep*

"shhh shhhhhh shsh shush shush"

The Night Watch Man's Tale

Some Things were gathering on the Path
What they were I couldn't say
Their eyes were large and roundly set
Their heads were flat, a diamond shape

They moved about in spindly pose
Lights lit the sky, I turned in fright
And saw a huge four windowed orb
Flashing through the moonlit night

I feared the Things were Aliens!
I sought escape… and to my shame
I told them I was Dracula!
They seemed to recognise the name

…They echoed it in fear and awe!!
AH! I knew my ploy had worked when they
…cleared the Path to let me through
And hurried QUICKLY on my way

Mad March Hare

Dear Mad March Hare…
… Wildly hopping through
The meadow…
All that frenzied jumping, kicking!!…

…Why don't you
Wear a gum shield, sir,
To stop your teeth a'clicking?"

"Well,…I did once wear
A gum shield
But my teeth became quite cross
They refused to
Chew a lettuce
Just to show me who was boss!

No, my teeth
Won't wear a gum shield;
They prefer to be out sticking
But still and all, and wherewithal
I thank you for your thinking

Notes on a Daring Rescue

Three little Herrings were netted one day
To be pickled and put in a can
When their sister found out she plotted
A so daring rescue plan
She asked a neighbourly Sword Fish
To open the net with his snout
Whilst a friendly Shark kept intruders at bay
By circling slowly about

And that's how those three little Herrings
Were rescued, with flair and élan
By their Sis and the Shark and the Swordfish
From the clutch of the cannery man

An Apology from the Shepherd's Union

Some ancient
Unknown shepherd
Boobed

A boob
We are bound to
Admitting

He mistakenly named
One sheep
A sheep

When a shoop
Would have been
Much More fitting

Persian Cat

A White Persian Cat
With Emerald Green eyes
Bought a House by a Silvery Bay
The resident Mouse
(A poor little thing)
Begged the Cat for permission to stay

The White Persian Cat
With a heart of pure gold
Granted the Mouse stay of leave
And the resident Mouse
Unpacked her bags
And breathed a deep sigh of relief

The White Persian Cat
And the resident Mouse
Lived in the friendliest way
Taking care of each other
The rest of their days
In the house by the Silvery Bay.

The Grateful Page

A puzzled Glow Worm
Spent his life
Wondering why he shone.

And why he didn't
Shine so much
When the lights were on

He never found
The answer,
And perhaps it's just as well,

Or I would be
An Empty Page,
Without a Tale to Tell

Pill Bugs

 Let's hear it for those Thingummy Things
Flat, grey, round, no bones
Who crawl in knowing symmetry
Beneath dank bricks and stones

Those 14 legged Thingummy Things
Who shun the arid light,
Sharp cousins of the Sea Bugs
Who breathe well through gills alike

Let's Honour them their hardiness
Their will to carry on
Why! Thingummy Things were crawling round
Ere Mankind came along!!!

So…
If you come upon, whilst digging,
The Pill Bugs' ancient home
Pray honour them their privacy
And leave no upturned stone.

Thank you, from P.B.s

The Militant Aphid

An Aphid living on a rose
Wished with all his mind
He owned a little tin of paint
You know, the spray-on kind

Then, whenever he was threatened
With an Aerosol Attack,
He could aim that little tin of paint
And spray The Gardener back.
Tee hee

Pondering Question

Now here is a
Pondering question
Thrown out to one and to all
If there's no such things
As Fairies
How come we all know they are small?

See, if there's no such
Things as Fairies
Or Elves or Pixies or things,
The question begs
To be answered
How come we all know they have wings?

And why do we all
Look for sixpence
In exchange for a Pillowed tooth?
AND... if there's no such
Things as Fairies
Who makes our wishes come true?

Believe, believe

The Hypochondriac

As I'm
Sweeping Up
The dust
I do so,
Reverently…

Always bearing
Well
In mind
Some of it
Is ME.

The Time Machine

A Time Machine landed in Mouseville
Out stepped a travelling Cat

He informed the crowding curious Mice
That the World was round, not flat…

…That the Moon was made of something else
Other than Blue Cheese
Pigs couldn't fly and Money
Didn't grow on Trees

The Cat swelled with importance
But as he paused for breath
A Flying Pig alighted
With a parcel round her neck

"I have a present from the Moon
A lump of cheese," she cried
"Fine Danish blue!" The Astronaut
Could not believe his eyes

The grinning Mice then pointed out
Rich Money trees galore!!
And the dazed Cat wondered if he'd travelled
Sideways…or back or forth

Trafalgar Square

I saw an old lady a'nodding her head
Which I brought her attention to bear
"Excuse me, your head keeps on nodding"
Oh! She gave me a pondering stare

"Of course I'm a'nodding and nodding
It's a habit of which I'm aware,
'tis a thing I picked up from the Pigeons
Whom I feed every day in the Square

"When I see those agreeable Pigeons
Nod nodding with nary a care
I think it unfriendly to not nod nod back
And the habit's stayed with me my dear"

A £1

A digging Mole dug up a £1
He couldn't believe his eyes
He showed it to his Mother
O! she fainted in surprise

He showed it to his Moley peers,
He showed it to his betters
Some turned green with envy,
A few wrote begging letters!

Two hundred Moles, that weekend,
Went digging underground
Feverishly hoping
To find another £1

So the moral of this tale, Mole,
As you dig and delve,
If you find another £1 lad
Keep it to yourself.

Two Spiteful Mice

A Cheshire cat lost
Two front teeth
At cricket, by a batter
Well, as he couldn't
See himself
He thought it didn't matter

Two spiteful mice
Thought otherwise
And to correct his error
They did a very
Spiteful thing
And sent that cat a mirror

And two large white Piano keys
With a pot of Polyfilla

At Pie Tom's

I'm proud to say
I'm a Yorkshire Cat
An honour if you please
And I make a crust
(As all Cats must)
Selling pie and peas

I'm proud to say
I'm a Yorkshire Mouse
An honour in my eyes
And I use great skill
(As all mice will)
Snaffling Pie Tom's pies

The Windfall

In a windy Orchard
Beneath an apple tree
A little queue of Maggots
Waiting patiently

A hopeful queue of Maggots
Weathering the storm
Waiting for a windfall
So they can set up home

Waiting for the wind to bring
That fruit from overhead
So they can set up Home lad

In apples **russet red**

Moonlight Mischief

 The Moon was out
And all was still…
Save for the sound of muffled taps
T'was thirteen Mice,
In silent mode
Intently nailing down the Cat Flaps

Dawn approached,
The Cats came home
Each to a nailed down flap door
And thirteen Mice
In silent glee
Sat back to watch the uproar. Tee hee

THE CONKERER

This Siamese cat is about to commence
Teaching young Conkers
The art of defence
    BOW LOW

With a whoop and a kick and a spin on one toe
He will teach them the art
Of evading a blow
    JUST SO

Aye, a whoop and a kick and a few uppercuts
Show the way of the Dragon
To young Conker Nuts
    GUNG HO

O! the art of defence 'tis a wonderful thing!
And essential for Conkers
Who fight from a string.
    AH SO

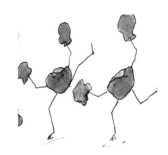

Of Possible Interest to Somconc

Twenty lazy schoolboys,
Yawning (as they do)
Wishing it was tea time,
Wishing school was through.
Glaring at the teacher…
When, to their surprise
He turned into a Rabbit
Before their very eyes!!!

He turned into a Rabbit,
Gave a little grin
Pointed to the blackboard,
Then turned back again
And twenty silent schoolboys,
Upright at their desk
Viewed that tricky teacher
With awe and great respect

Silence in the classroom!
Now teacher rules the roost
(Metamorphosing now and then,
To give his cred a boost)
Twenty model schoolboys!!
You too could reach that end
…if you turn into a rabbit sir,
Every now and then.

The Conscientious Bookbinder

I bind my books in leather soft
My gilding is the best
And all prospective bookworms
Must pass a spelling test

Yes all prospective bookworms
Must pass this test for me
The worms I bind inside my books
Must be quite literate you see

Those worms who have a versey bent
I bind in books of prose
The dictionary I reserve
For worms who prove verbose

The worms who are, oh, worldy wise
In atlases are bound
The bookworms who love gossip
In diaries are found

And the bookworms with no culture
You know, no feel for words
I bind them up in bacon rind
And give them to the birds.

Printed in Poland
by Amazon Fulfillment
Poland Sp. z o.o., Wrocław